GOOD

The Swimming Hole

by
Cam Higgins

illustrated by
Ariel Landy

LITTLE SIMON

New York London Toronto Sydney New Delhi

LITTLE SIMON
An imprint of Simon & Schuster Children's Publishing Division
1230 Avenue of the Americas, New York, New York 10020
First Little Simon paperback edition July 2021
Copyright © 2021 by Simon & Schuster, Inc.
Also available in a Little Simon hardcover edition.
All rights reserved, including the right of reproduction in whole or in part in any form. LITTLE SIMON is a registered trademark of Simon & Schuster, Inc., and associated colophon is a trademark of Simon & Schuster, Inc.
For information about special discounts for bulk purchases, please contact Simon & Schuster Special Sales at 1-866-506-1949 or business@simonandschuster.com.
The Simon & Schuster Speakers Bureau can bring authors to your live event. For more information or to book an event contact the Simon & Schuster Speakers Bureau at 1-866-248-3049 or visit our website at www.simonspeakers.com.
Designed by Leslie Mechanic
Manufactured in the United States of America 0822 MTN
10 9 8 7 6 5 4 3 2
Library of Congress Cataloging-in-Publication Data
Names: Higgins, Cam, author. | Landy, Ariel, illustrator. Title: The swimming hole / by Cam Higgins; illustrated by Ariel Landy. Description: First Little Simon edition. | New York: Little Simon, 2021. | Series: Good dog; #5 | Audience: Ages 5–9. | Summary: Scrapper teaches Bo to swim when they visit the swimming hole with their human family.
Identifiers: LCCN 2020051555 (print) | LCCN 2020051556 (ebook) | ISBN 9781534495340 (paperback) | ISBN 9781534495357 (hardcover) | ISBN 9781534495364 (ebook)   Subjects: CYAC: Sheep dogs—Fiction. | Dogs—Fiction. | Swimming—Fiction. | Farm life—Fiction. | Friendship—Fiction.
Classification: LCC PZ7.1.H54497 Swi 2021 (print) | LCC PZ7.1.H54497 (ebook) | DDC [E]—dc23
LC record available at https://lccn.loc.gov/2020051555

CONTENTS

Made in
the Shade

Every farm has a big tree.

You know, a huge one with wide limbs perfect for human kids to climb. One that you can't miss.

Sometimes the tree is next to the barn. Sometimes it's in front of the house.

The big tree on our farm is in the middle of the field. On hot days, everyone gathers there.

Why? you might ask. Because the big tree gives the absolute best and coolest shade.

Every animal on the farm needs shade on hot summer days. The cats stay in the barn, horses stay in their stalls, and pigs stay in the mud—if they are lucky enough to find a pool of mud.

But when it is so hot that it feels like the sun is tapping you on the back, the best place to be is under the big tree.

All the animals meet there, and it's like a party. Well, it's more like a slumber party, because everybody likes to close their eyes and enjoy the sweet breeze.

One sunny day, a young bird perched in the branches of the big tree and began singing.

I liked his song. It went like this: "Tweetly tweet tweet, sweetly tweet tweet twee."

Billy the goat, on the other hand, did not like the song. He did not like it at all.

So Billy did what any goat would do. He climbed into the big tree. I'd never seen that before—it was pretty neat!

The bird didn't think it was so cool, though. He flew away with a squawk and left Billy up in the branches all by himself.

The other animals cheered. I guess they didn't like the birdsong either.

"Now we can all get some rest," Billy announced proudly.

Then he looked around, as if noticing for the first time that he was up in a tree.

"But first, could someone help me?" Billy asked.

The animals looked at one another, and it was clear. We had no idea how to get that goat down.

Hot,
Hot, Hot

But I knew who could help Billy: Nanny Sheep! She's the smartest animal I know!

I ran through the field to find her resting by the barn.

"Hey, Nanny Sheep! Billy the goat climbed the big tree to keep a bird from singing, and he's stuck!" I told her.

"Oh, that poor young bird, getting bullied by a grumpy billy goat," she said. "I will help, but Billy must apologize to the little one."

When we reached the big tree, Billy was perched on a wide, low limb. And he looked scared.

"Billy," Nanny Sheep called. "The first step to climbing down safely is listening to me very carefully, okay?"

Billy nodded, but the expression on his face didn't change.

Nanny Sheep waved to Comet, a young foal.

"Comet, would you please stand below this branch?" Nanny Sheep asked.

"Of course," said Comet.

"Thank you, dear," said Nanny Sheep. Then she turned to Billy and said, "Time for the second step. Reach down with your back leg until you can stand on Comet's back."

Other sheep gathered around Comet to catch Billy just in case he fell.

Billy took a deep breath. He shifted one leg carefully, then quickly moved it back.

"Oh, I can't do it!" he moaned.

"Billy, you have to trust your friends," Nanny Sheep calmly told him. "We will keep you safe, as long as you listen and believe in us."

The goat closed his eyes and stretched for Comet's back once again.

"You need to move lower," Comet called up to Billy.

"It's impossible!" he shouted. "I'm too scared!"

"You are a very brave goat, Billy," said Nanny Sheep. "If you don't get it right the first or second time you try, take a break. We will get you out of that tree—just don't give up."

I could see Billy relax at Nanny's words. He lifted his leg again, and this time, he found Comet's broad back.

"Wonderful, Billy!" Nanny Sheep said. "Now lower your other leg."

Billy tried to move and lost his balance.

The whole barnyard gasped as he wobbled!

Luckily, Billy quickly caught himself and soon had two feet on Comet's back. Then slowly, step by step, Billy was out of the tree!

We all gave him a cheer for a job
well done, but now Billy had a new
task. He needed to apologize to the
young bird he chased away.

He walked all around
the farm searching for
the right bird with
Nanny Sheep. I
followed them too,
just in case Billy
got stuck in any
more trees.

When I got home at the end of the
day, I was hot, hot, hot. But as soon as
the door swung open,
a blast of cold air met
me, ruffling my fur. It
was *brrr*-ific!

I headed straight for the kitchen floor. It's the best place to plop down after a hot day. The tiles are cool against your belly, and you can let your tongue flap out as you catch your breath.

Imani sat down next to me and said, "Wow, Bo, I think you need a cooldown trip tomorrow. How does that sound?"

She scratched behind my ears, and I rested my head in her lap. I was way more excited on the inside than I seemed on the outside. But I was wiped out. This heat had me beat.

GO,
GO, GO

The next morning, I woke up to find Imani and Wyatt downstairs in the kitchen.

They were dressed in bathing suits and were busy stuffing fluffy towels and sunscreen into their backpacks.

Oh, I like sunscreen. It smells so yummy, even if it's not food.

My human parents, Jennica and Darnell, were there too. They were packing a cooler with water, juice boxes, snacks, and sandwiches!

Suddenly the smell of salami and bacon and peanut butter filled the air, and my tail started wagging. Plus, I started drooling a little—just a little.

And I knew those sandwiches weren't for me. But something big was going on. When your family packs a picnic, you know you're going on a big adventure!

"Well, well, look who's finally awake," Wyatt said. "Come on, sleepyhead Bo, we're going to the swimming hole today."

The swimming hole? What was that? Was it the cooldown trip Imani talked about last night?

I licked Wyatt's hand, then heard a familiar sound. Darnell was filling my dish with kibble! He also placed a nice, cold bowl of water beside it.

"Eat up first," Darnell said. "You can't go hiking on an empty stomach."

He didn't have to tell me twice. I dug in, and once I finished, we were off.

It was hot that morning. Hotter than it was yesterday. I woofed to the sheep who were grazing in the meadow as they watched us head into the woods. A few of the sheep even baaed back!

I love the woods. As soon as we stepped under the trees, the world got a little cooler.

We walk in the woods all the time, but that day, Imani told me that we were going to take a different path.

"It's time you visited the swimming hole, boy!" she cheered.

There was that name again: the swimming hole. Maybe it was part of the old creek? That place was great! The water was cold and not too deep at all. I could walk in up to my knees and watch the tiny minnows swim past. I love to splash through the creek every summer.

But the creek was in the opposite direction. Hmm, guess this swimming hole was somewhere else.

We hiked for a long time in and out of the hot sun. I saw lizards. I saw squirrels. I even saw the young bird Billy the goat chased out of the tree. But I did not see a swimming hole.

Then I finally heard the sound of people splashing and laughing. We walked around a corner, and the forest opened up to reveal what had to be the swimming hole.

There was a little beach with soft dirt that led down to a lake with tree branches dipping low over the water. There was plenty of room for swimming, but the water looked deep and dark.

I trotted over for a closer look. I couldn't see the bottom of the swimming hole—Woof! I couldn't see anything in the water except for my own reflection.

A nervous feeling started in my belly. Splashing around close to shore was fun, but this was clearly a place for swimming.

Then I heard a new sound—it was a dog barking! And I knew that bark anywhere! It was my best friend, Scrapper. And he was running across the beach . . . right toward me.

Swinging, Swimming

"Woof! Woof! Hey, Bo!" Scrapper called out as he hopped around in a happy circle. "I didn't know you were coming today! This is so great!"

My tail wagged and wagged.

"It sure is!" I agreed.

Then Scrapper bounced over to the water.

"Last one in is a rotten pup!" he said.

"Wait!" I cried. "I, uh, I should wait

for Wyatt and Imani to get ready and come in too."

"Oh, okay," Scrapper said.

We found the others and followed
along as they helped their parents set
up the blanket and towels.

Then Imani, Wyatt, and Scrapper's
human brother, Hank, headed *away*
from the water.

Hmm, that was very mysterious!
Didn't we come to the swimming hole
to swim . . . in the swimming hole?

Luckily, Scrapper and I were on the
case!

We trailed the kids down a path that led to an old tire at the side of the lake. It looked very out of place. What did an old tire have to do with the swimming hole?

Well, I found out soon enough.

The tire was attached to a rope that was tied to a thick branch higher up in the tree. Imani grabbed the tire, stood up on it, and then swung away!

Oh, wow—it was a tire swing! Not only that, but it was a tire swing that flew out over the swimming hole! Imani gave a whooping cheer as she let go of the swing and splashed down into the water below.

Next, Hank climbed onto the tire and did a flip off the swing, landing with a belly flop and a huge splash. Wyatt and Imani both laughed loudly and cheered for Hank. After a moment, his head popped up out of the water, and he yelled, "Beat that, Wyatt!"

Now it was Wyatt's turn to swing out over the swimming hole, but he didn't let go. Nope, he swung back over the land, then over the swimming hole again. He pumped and pumped, sending the tire swing higher and higher.

Scrapper and I watched as the tire swing started to bounce up and down. I growled nervously. What if the branch snapped?

But then Wyatt let go of the tire and dove into the water with the biggest splash.

The kids all laughed and clapped loudly. Scrapper and I howled with joy.

But there was one sneaky animal who kept quiet: a squirrel!

He climbed out onto the branch with the tire swing and sniffed the rope.

I didn't know what that squirrel was up to, but I'm sure it was no good. I let out a growl, but then Scrapper stopped me.

"Aw, leave him alone, Bo," he said. "It's too hot to chase squirrels. C'mon, let's go get in that water!"

Um, too hot to chase squirrels? What was Scrapper talking about? But before I could say a word, Scrapper called, "Race you back to the beach!"

He took off running, and even though I probably should have stayed to deal with that squirrel, I couldn't resist a good race.

Wet Slime

The two of us ran as fast as we could around the lake.

Scrapper was ahead of me most of the way, but then I found a shortcut over a fallen tree in the forest path. We made it to the beach at the exact same time. It was a tie, but only just barely.

"Aw, I thought I finally had you," said Scrapper.

"Well, you *did* have a head start," I reminded him.

Scrapper nodded in agreement. "I guess so."

We looked out over the water and could see the kids not too far away.

They had already come back up to the beach and grabbed their floats. They were smiling and talking happily in the water; they looked like they were having a great time.

"Come on, let's go join them!" Scrapper cheered as he darted into the water.

Soon he was up to his neck and
paddling like a champ. He swam in
circles, calling to me.

"Come on, Bo!"

"I'm coming, I'm coming," I called
out. "Hold your seahorses!"

I put one paw in the water. It was ice-cold and exactly what I needed for my hot puppy toes after the long hike here. But then I noticed a different feeling. The bottom of the swimming hole wasn't sandy like the beach. And it wasn't rocky like the creek. It was slimy!

"Yuck! I stepped on something slippy-slimy gross!" I whined.

I jerked my paw back out of the water, and something was hanging from it! It was green and wet and totally stuck to me! I shook my paw to get it off.

But the more it shook, the worse it got. It stuck to my leg, then to my tail, and then to my nose!

In no time, I must have looked like a sea monster!

"Oh, that? Yeah, don't worry about that," said Scrapper. "It's normal. Just start swimming, and you won't even have to touch it."

After I took a quick roll in the dirt, the green gunk came off. Now it was time to tell the truth.

"Um, Scrapper," I said, "I have to say something, and I don't want you to tease me about it."

"Tease you?" asked Scrapper.
"Friends don't do that. Just tell me
what's up, pup!"

"It's just that I, uh, don't know how to swim," I said.

Scrapper swam back immediately with a big smile on his face. "Why didn't you say so? Because you just happen to know one of the best swimmers around—me!"

Doggy– Paddle

Scrapper swam back to the beach and shook the water off. Unfortunately, it got all over me.

When he finished, he cleared his throat and made an announcement. "First things first. I'll be your swim instructor, so please listen to what I tell you."

I nodded my head uncertainly. "Okay. But I'm a little bit scared."

"That's all right, Bo," he said. "It's normal to feel anxious and scared. But I won't let anything happen to you, as long as you listen to me and try to do what I tell you."

"Okay," I said reluctantly.

"Let's start with floating," Scrapper said as he stepped back in. "Arch your back, then swirl your paws in the water. It's easy!"

Hmm, he did make it look easy. So I decided to give it a try.

Big mistake!

I stepped back in the swimming hole
and slipped on the wet slime. Instead of
floating, I splashed myself in the face
and took in a big mouthful of water.

"Scrapper, I can't do it!" I whimpered
as I struggled back to the beach.

"Yes, you can. Just keep trying," Scrapper said patiently. "Remember to swirl your paws and push your back up toward the sky. If you do that, then you won't slip on that gross green goo."

I tried again, but my paws just didn't seem to know which way to go, and I could feel myself sinking.

"Maybe swimming isn't my thing," I spluttered angrily after another dunk underwater.

Scrapper smiled. "Keep working at it, Bo. You'll get it. Not all pups swim on their very first time in the water, or even their second or third. You just have to keep trying."

But no matter how hard I tried, I just couldn't do it. My legs were getting tired, my paws were getting goopy, and even my tail was sore.

I think Scrapper could tell, too, because he suggested we take a break.

So I slumped back to the shore and plopped down on the Davis family's blanket, feeling like an awfully silly pup.

Cats
and Water

As I rested, Scrapper and the kids splashed and laughed in the distance. I could tell they were having a great time.

Even Darnell called out for me to join them in the lake.

"Hey, Bo! Come on in!" he shouted happily. "The water's fine!"

He looked like a mountain floating in the water, so big and strong.

I wanted to stand up, but my poor legs had other ideas. I dropped back down. Maybe a little more rest would help.

Then I heard another voice . . . and it came from the bushes behind me.

"*Psst,*" someone hissed.

"Who's there?" I asked, looking around.

I noticed four gleaming eyes and two sneaky smiles. It was King and Diva, the barn cats.

What were they doing all the way out here, so far from the farm?

As they turned their sly grins my way, I realized exactly what they were doing out here. They had come to make fun of me.

"Hey, Diva, what's wet and soggy and stinks like a froggy?" King asked.

Diva snorted with laughter. "Oh, I know! Is it the same little puppy who thinks he's a guppy, but can't even doggy-paddle?"

Oh, my fur stood on end! But I couldn't let them know they were making me upset. That's exactly what those cats wanted.

"I thought cats and water don't mix," I woofed back.

"Oh, we're not here to swim, Bo," said King. "We're here for the sun."

Both cats stretched out and rolled over in the soft grass just beside the sand of the beach. I felt the warmth of the sun too, and it *did* feel good.

"But if we wanted to swim, we could," said Diva. "Because while cats don't *like* water, at least we're not *afraid* of it . . . like some pups."

Well, that was all I could take. I knew I'd get in trouble for chasing those cats, but what was a poor puppy to do? I stood on the edge of the blanket and dug my tired paws into the sand.

"You take that back," I told them.

"Or what?" asked King. "You'll bark and chase us? We're just innocent cats lying in the sun. You're the *bad dog* that tried to bite us."

I could feel the biggest, loudest bark ever rising up in my throat. I was about to open my mouth to let it out when the strangest thing happened.

A tiny acorn plunked down right on King's head.

"Ouch!" snapped King. "What was that?"

Then another acorn dropped on Diva's paw. "Ack! My perfect nails!"

More acorns rained down from above, landing softly in the grass and sand, and also bonking the cats, which sent them quickly running away into the forest.

I expected to see Scrapper shaking the trunk to bring down the acorns. But nope, he was still swimming with the kids.

Then I looked up into the tree, and guess what I saw? A squirrel!

It was the same squirrel I had seen on the tire swing. I was sure of it—I never forgot a squirrel face.

He was balanced on a branch holding a stack of acorns in his little arms, ready to throw them down on the cats.

I was really confused now. Why would a squirrel ever help a dog? But before I had a chance to ask, he squeaked and bounded away.

8
Picnic,
Picnic

I thought about chasing the squirrel.
Sure, I think about chasing squirrels
a lot, but this time I just wanted to talk
to him. There were a million questions
running through my mind.

But then Jennica called us over for
something that I could not ignore.
"Picnic time!"

Every pup knew what that meant. It was time to eat!

I raced over to see what everyone had brought. There was such a wonderful feast laid out on the beach blanket. I spotted a big bowl of tortilla chips and salsa. There were giant platters of potato salad and macaroni salad.

There was even a sandwich-making station with slices of different breads and salami and ham and turkey and cheese and even jars of peanut butter and jelly and wow, it smelled yummy!

Plus, Jennica had made her prizewinning peach-blueberry pie for dessert.

Oh, all the smells were yum-yum-yummy!

"Ah, ah, ah," said Imani as she stepped between the pie and me. "This is all people food, remember?"

Now, of course my brain knew that, but my stomach was a different story. I tried not to drool, but I couldn't stop myself.

"Don't worry, Bo," Jennica told me.
"I baked special *pupcakes* for you and
Scrapper."

I had no idea what pupcakes were,

but I didn't care one bit.

Everything Jennica
made was delicious!

The humans filled their plates as Scrapper and I dug into a pile of kibble that Scrapper's family brought along for us. Then we drank some ice-cold water that was frosty and refreshing.

I might have spilled more than I drank, I was so thirsty.

And finally, it was pupcake time!

"Here you go, boys," Jennica said as she set our food down on the blanket.

Here's one way Scrapper and I are different. He's a pup who eats things all in a rush, without even thinking about it. He gobbled up his pupcake in just one bite!

But not me. I'm a pup who likes to make my treats last as long as possible.

First, I gave my pupcake the sniff test. Oooh, I could smell peanut butter . . . and banana . . . and even a hint of bacon!

Next, I gave it the lick test to get a hint of the flavor. I licked the pupcake and WOW! It tasted like fireworks in my mouth, all yummy and fantastic and bright.

By that time, Scrapper had had enough. "JUST EAT THE YUMMY THING ALREADY!"

"I would if you didn't interrupt me," I told him. "It's not like the pupcake is going to run away."

Let me tell you, I wished I hadn't said that, because guess what. My pupcake actually ran away! And it ran away fast!

"See? I told you," said Scrapper. "You've got to eat your food quickly, or else it will escape."

Then I spotted a very fluffy tail underneath my very speedy pupcake.

"It's not escaping!" I yelled. "It's being stolen . . . by that squirrel!"

Squirrel
Overboard

The chase was on! I dashed after that squirrel, but he was fast! He let go of my pupcake, hoping I would stop running after him, but I didn't stop.

No, sir. If you are going to chase a squirrel, you have to chase it until the job is done. The minute you give up, the squirrel wins.

We made it all the way to the tire swing, and that's when I knew I had a chance to catch him. The squirrel leaped onto the tire, and I jumped into action.

I pushed the swing with my front
paws, and it went twirling in circles
out over the water.

Oh boy, I had that squirrel trapped!

I watched as the squirrel spun and spun until he slipped off the swing and fell into the swimming hole!

Oh, no! Can squirrels even swim?

Without even thinking, I leaped
into the water to help. My legs had a
mind of their own.

I landed with a splash, and as
the water came up around me, I
remembered I kind of couldn't swim.

Luckily, Scrapper had followed me to the swing. He called out from above. "Bo! Remember our doggy-paddle lesson!"

Then he barked all the steps he had told me to do earlier.

I tried to calm down and pay attention. It reminded me of Nanny Sheep's advice for Billy. I listened to Scrapper's instructions, to move my paws, arch my back, and keep my head above the water.

And do you know what? After a
moment, I was swimming! My front
paws were paddling and my back legs
were kicking. Sure, I wasn't the best
swimmer, but I was doing it.

I paddled over to the squirrel,
and guess what. That squirrel could
already swim!

I suppose that made sense if you live next to a swimming hole.

The two of us swam to safety, just as Wyatt and Imani ran over to see if I was okay.

Here's a doggy secret: I was better than okay. I was great—because I was swimming!

The Swimming Hole

We enjoyed the rest of the day in the warm sunshine, swimming and playing with our friends.

I doggy-paddled all around the swimming hole with Scrapper, Imani, Wyatt, and Hank. We played all kinds of games in the water: chasing games, racing games, and floating games.

Plus, Scrapper taught me how to dive! Well, maybe my dives were more like graceful belly flops. Either way, jumping into the lake was so much fun!

This was a perfect day. I couldn't imagine what could have made it better, but then Jennica brought out an extra pupcake for me! This time, when she placed it in front of me, I ate it faster than fast. Yum!

"Smart move, buddy," said Scrapper.
"You never know when that sneaky
squirrel is going to strike again."

114

I would have agreed with him, but
my mouth was totally full of banana,
peanut butter, bacon, and cakey
goodness.

But Scrapper was right. Squirrels were mysterious creatures. I still couldn't figure out why that squirrel would help me with the cats, but then steal my pupcake. It made no sense at all. I guess squirrels don't need to make sense. . . . That's what makes them squirrels.

Oh well, there's no time to worry about squirrel friends when I've got my favorite splash friends right here!

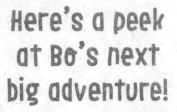

Here's a peek at Bo's next big adventure!

GOOD D🐾G 6

Life Is Good

There was something in the air. Something new, with a sharp, tangy smell. All of us could sense it.

The chicks were waddling a little faster. The sheep grew a bit fluffier. The pigs—well, they always eat . . . but they started eating a lot more.

An excerpt from *Life Is Good*

It all started one chilly morning when a wisp of white cloud blew right out of my mouth. I was outside with Wyatt and Imani, my human brother and sister, while they were doing their daily chores on the farm.

I stopped in my tracks as soon as I saw that first white puff. I was so surprised! It looked super yummy, so I opened my mouth wide. But it disappeared before I could bite it.

"Bo!" Imani laughed as she watched me chase the white puffs. "Silly dog, that's your own breath. When it's cold out, you can see your

An excerpt from *Life Is Good*

breath when you breathe out. Here, watch."

Imani blew out a big white cloud that floated in the air. She looked like a fire-breathing dragon from one of those books she liked to read. Hmm, did this mean Imani could breathe real fire too? I hoped not!

"Looks like we're in for a cold snap," said Wyatt. "Maybe it will even snow!"

Imani jumped toward the sky and cheered. "Oooh, I sure hope so!"

An excerpt from *Life Is Good*